Quarto Knows

Quarto is the authority on a wide range of topics.
Quarto educates, entertains, and enriches the lives of our readers—
enthusiasts and lovers of hands-on living.
www.quartoknows.com

Illustrated by Stephanie Peterson Jones
Written by Hannah Klaus Hunter

Walter Foster Jr.

6 Orchard Road, Suite 100
Lake Forest, CA 92630
quartoknows.com
Visit our blogs @quartoknows.com

FSC
www.fsc.org

MIX
Paper from
responsible sources
FSC® C016973

Printed in China
1 3 5 7 9 10 8 6 4 2

Table of Contents

How to Use This Book........... 6

Coloring Sections

Earth 9

Air 29

Fire 49

Water 69

Free Drawing 88

Letter to Parents 93

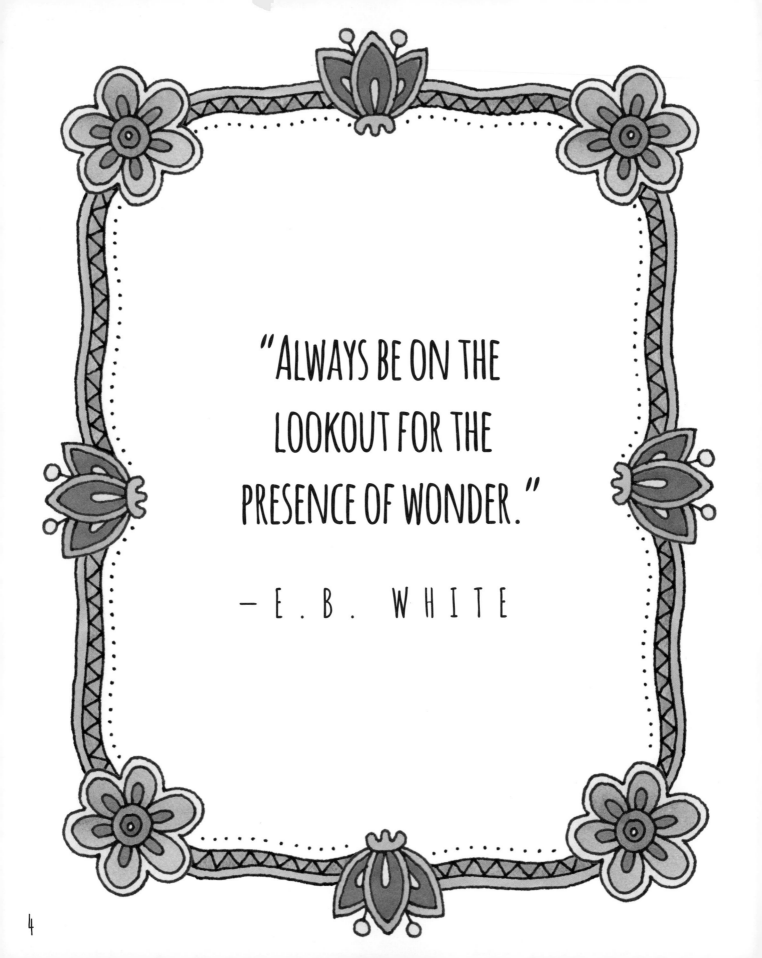

"ALWAYS BE ON THE LOOKOUT FOR THE PRESENCE OF WONDER."

— E.B. WHITE

HOW TO USE THIS BOOK

This book is divided into sections: Earth, Air, Fire, Water, and Free Drawing. You get to decide where to begin, whether you want to use crayons, colored pencils, fat markers, or thin markers. Any of these will work perfectly—the choice is yours. Whatever medium you choose, there are also tips on choosing color and color mixing. Short quotes at the beginning of each section set the mood.

MATERIALS TO USE

- crayons
- colored pencils
- sketch book for copying pictures
- fat or thin markers
- tracing paper

A guide to the wonderful world of color:

The color wheel is a circle divided into slices, and it tells us about colors and how they relate to each other. Red, blue, and yellow are called primary colors because they can't be made by mixing any other colors. There are secondary colors too—orange, green, and purple. You can make each of those colors by mixing two primary colors together.

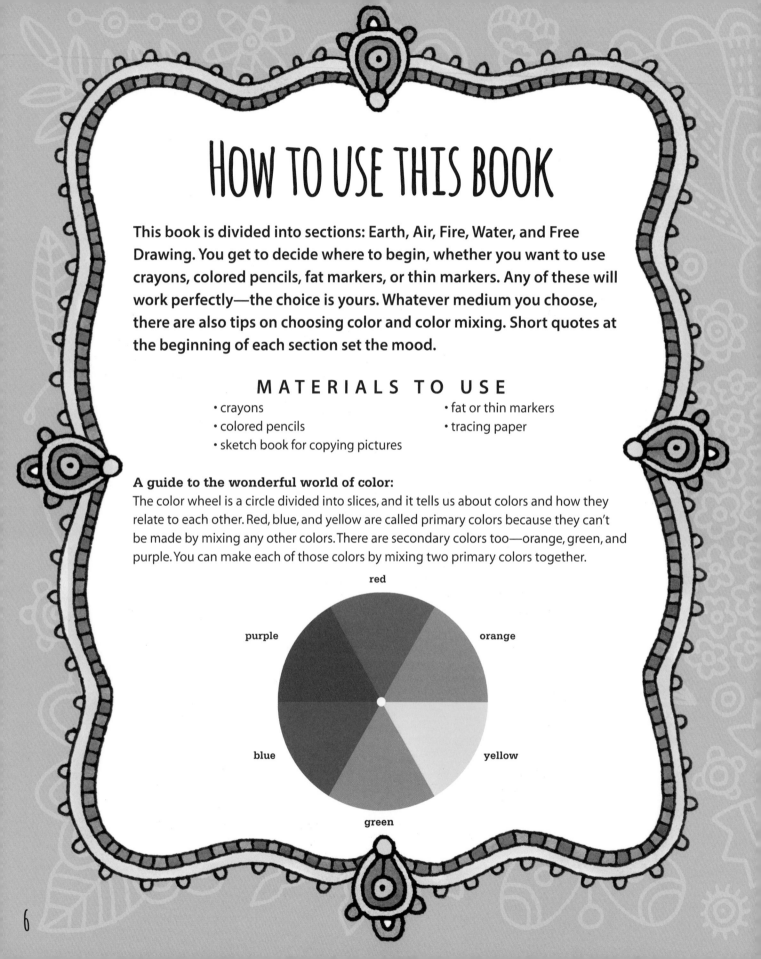

red

purple

orange

blue

yellow

green

We can also divide colors into warm and cool shades. Warm colors have more red and yellow in them. They include many shades of red, pink, orange, yellow, and red-purple. When we look at these colors, they make us feel warm, like a fire. Cool colors have more blue mixed into them and include some yellows, greens, blues, and violet blues. When we look at these colors, they might remind us of a lake or sky.

warm colors

cool colors

There is no right or wrong way to mix color. Colors are often linked to feelings. When deciding what color to use, you can ask yourself "how does this color make me feel?" **Experiment and find out how you can use color to express feelings.**

LINES AND COLOR

Have you ever heard someone say, "Don't color outside of the lines"? In this book, we want you to do just the opposite. You can start on the outside of the picture and color your way in, or you can begin in the center and color your way out. Add patterns or shapes if you like—dots, lines, zigzags, and triangles. As you've heard us say before, there's no right way to do this.

DOODLE AND DRAW

Finally, for those of you who want to learn to draw or improve your drawing skills, you can use this book as a template. Try tracing the picture to get the feel of the artist's lines. Once you have the lines down, you can use a piece of paper and a pencil to try copying it. Copying is a time-honored technique that artists have used for hundreds of years. However you choose to use this book, the main thing you need to know is **"Be Happy & Color!"**

EARTH

When we say Earth is our home, what do we mean?

Most of us live in houses or apartments, maybe even igloos, but all these homes are built on the surface of the earth. Earth is home to many creatures; every tree, flower, tiger, fish, or butterfly, if it could speak, would tell us Earth is their home too. Time for us to get to know some of our neighbors!

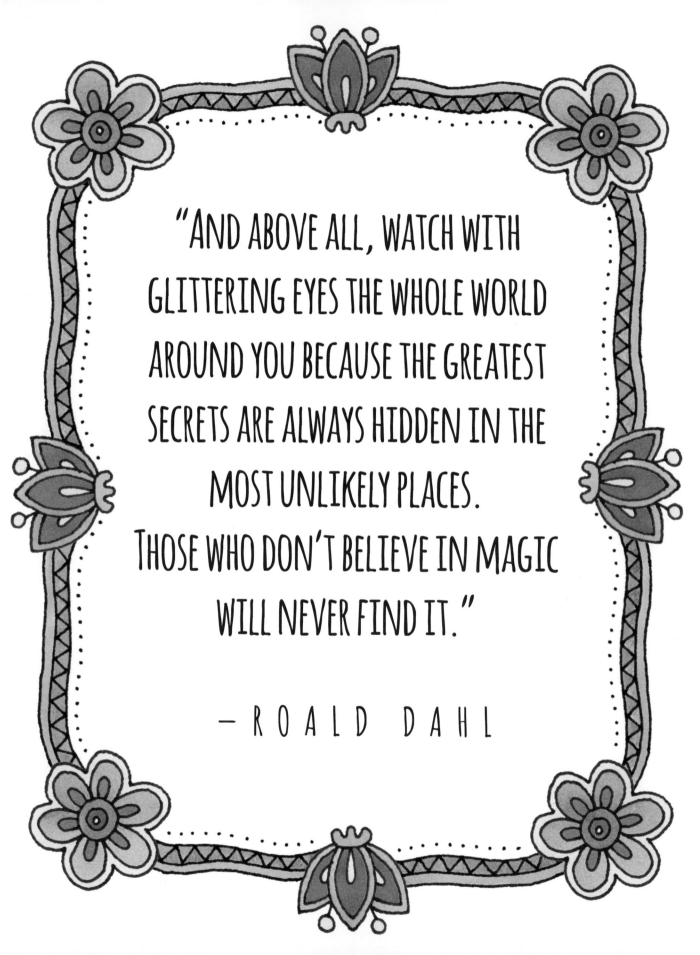

"And above all, watch with glittering eyes the whole world around you because the greatest secrets are always hidden in the most unlikely places. Those who don't believe in magic will never find it."

— ROALD DAHL

FLOWERS, LIKE PEOPLE, HAVE THEIR OWN LANGUAGE. COLOR EACH OF YOUR FLOWERS SO THAT THEY CAN SPEAK. WHAT WOULD EACH OF THEM SAY?

15

We're on a trip around the world! Our first stop is Antarctica, where you've just discovered a new species of penguin.

WHAT COLORS ARE THEY? THEY CAN BE ANY COLOR YOU WANT.
IF YOU'D LIKE, GIVE THEM A NAME.

Palm trees, butterflies, flowers, and ocean waves—it's all in the tropics!
And because it is yours, you can grow anything you want.
What does your tropical paradise look like?

WHAT ABOUT THE DESERT? ONE DESERT CREATURE IS THE RATTLESNAKE. IT HAS THE MOST AMAZING DESIGNS ON ITS BACK; DIAMONDS AND ZIGZAGS THAT HELP IT BLEND IN WITH ITS SURROUNDINGS. YOU CAN BE A TOP SNAKE DESIGNER TOO. DRAW A SNAKE WITH A COMPLETELY NEW PATTERN.

25

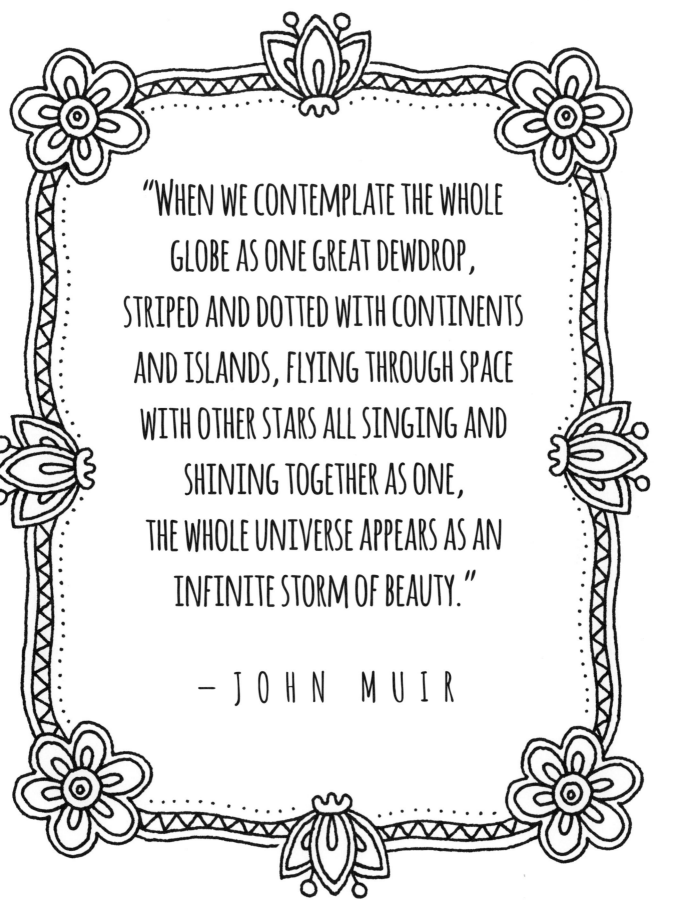

"WHEN WE CONTEMPLATE THE WHOLE GLOBE AS ONE GREAT DEWDROP, STRIPED AND DOTTED WITH CONTINENTS AND ISLANDS, FLYING THROUGH SPACE WITH OTHER STARS ALL SINGING AND SHINING TOGETHER AS ONE, THE WHOLE UNIVERSE APPEARS AS AN INFINITE STORM OF BEAUTY."

— JOHN MUIR

AIR

Have you ever thought about clouds, those pillow-like puffs of water droplets?

They're so light they float on air. There are many ways to explore clouds, whether you're seated on an airplane or perched on the ground. Try using some crayons and paper to draw the clouds as they float by. Or how about a rainbow—what would it look like if you were standing right in the middle of one?

"Clouds come floating
into my life,
no longer to carry
rain or usher storm,
but to add color
to my sunset sky."

– RABINDRANATH TAGORE

31

BUGS AND BUTTERFLIES COME IN A RAINBOW OF COLORS AND PATTERNS.
ON THIS PAGE, TRY USING CIRCLES AND CURVED LINES TO CREATE YOUR OWN
UNIQUE PATTERNS. WHAT COLORS DO YOU FEEL LIKE TODAY?
USE THOSE COLORS AS YOU DESIGN YOUR BUGS AND BUTTERFLIES.

Birds are creatures of the air. These two pages feature some familiar birds, but you get to choose exactly how they look. Have you ever seen a bird with a purple beak and green wings?

It is perfect kite-flying weather in this valley.
You are launching two of your favorite kites.
What shapes are you flying today?
Color your kites to fit your mood.

Before there were airplanes, people traveled in the air by balloon. Design your own balloon to travel up, up, and away. Use your favorite colors and patterns.

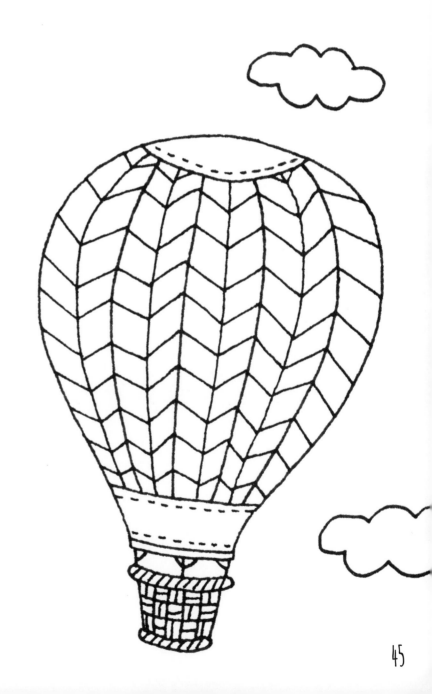

46

"LIVE IN THE SUNSHINE,
SWIM THE SEA,
DRINK THE WILD AIR."

— RALPH WALDO EMERSON

FIRE

**Have you ever sat around
a campfire or snuggled near a
fireplace on a cold winter night?**
Fire keeps us warm, just like the sun. We can
make fire ourselves, but it also lives deep inside
the earth, beneath the crust and in volcanic
mountains, sometimes spewing out as lava. Fire
brings light into darkness and is hot enough to
melt sand into glass. How different from water!
What kind of colors make you think of fire?

"Some painters transform the sun into a yellow spot, others transform a yellow spot into the sun."

– PABLO PICASSO

People often draw suns with faces,
just like the sun below.

TRY DRAWING A SUN WITH A DIFFERENT EXPRESSION.
WHAT WILL YOUR SUN LOOK LIKE?

54

If you could create your own planet, what would it look like?
Would it have colorful gases swirling around it?
Would there be rings? Draw the planet of your dreams.

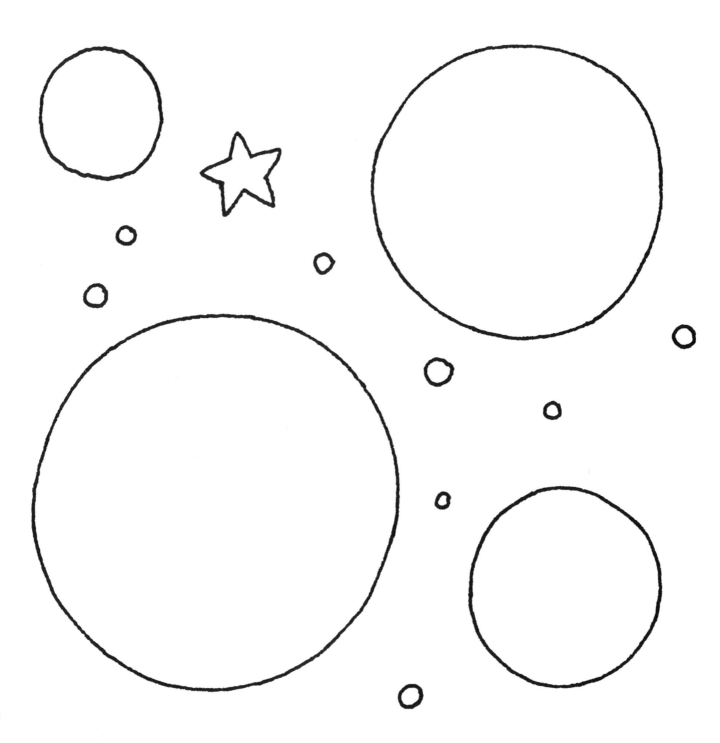

57

Imagine you're sitting on a big rock, looking up at the stars in the night sky. You can see all kinds of patterns in the stars. Can you draw them so that your friends can see them too?

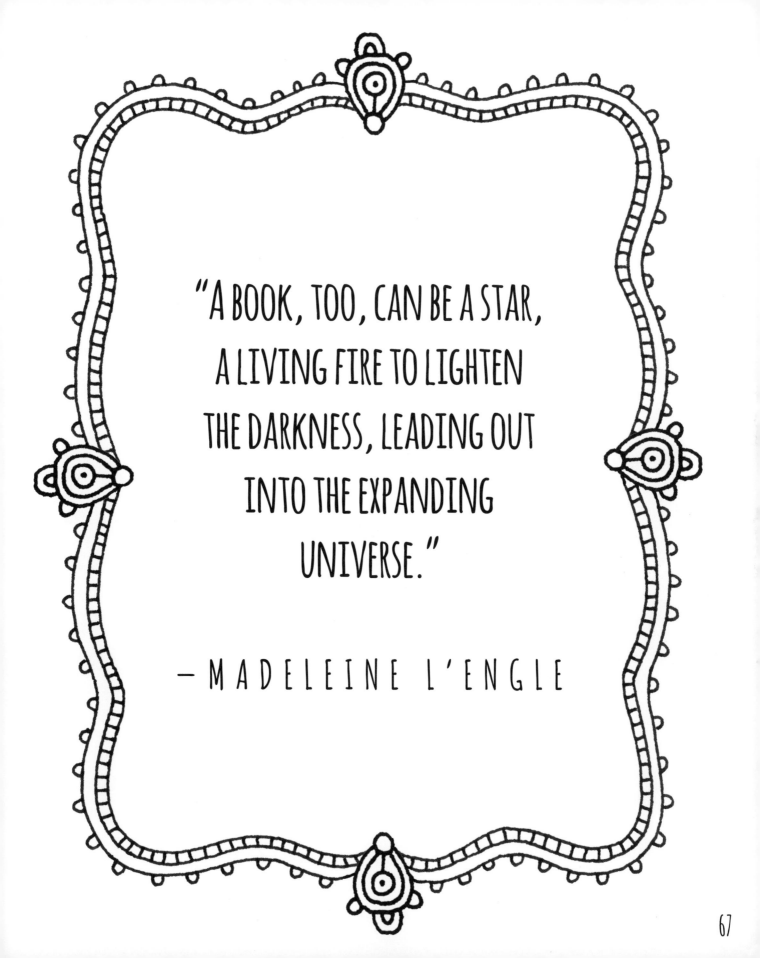

"A BOOK, TOO, CAN BE A STAR,
A LIVING FIRE TO LIGHTEN
THE DARKNESS, LEADING OUT
INTO THE EXPANDING
UNIVERSE."

— MADELEINE L'ENGLE

WATER

**Water comes in many forms:
rain, snow, or sleet.**

What do they all have in common?
Rain falls from the sky, and snow melts and
runs down mountains. Waterfalls cascade over
rocks and join with rivers, and all of these flow
into the sea. Water has amazing abilities: It wears
down rocks, carries ships across the sea, and
provides homes to millions of creatures. Last but
not least, water hydrates us. What colors do you
think of when you think of water?

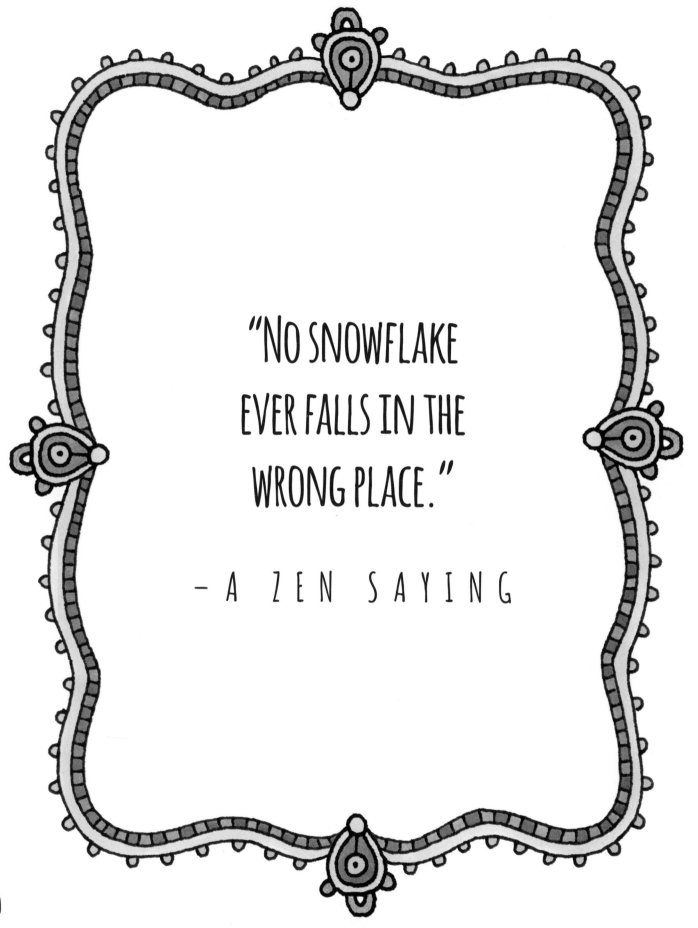

"NO SNOWFLAKE
EVER FALLS IN THE
WRONG PLACE."

– A ZEN SAYING

People say that, just like humans, no two snowflakes
are alike. It's true. Snowflake patterns are formed with crosses, arrows,
and circles. Try drawing a snowflake for each special person in your life.
The snowflakes can be any color you want.

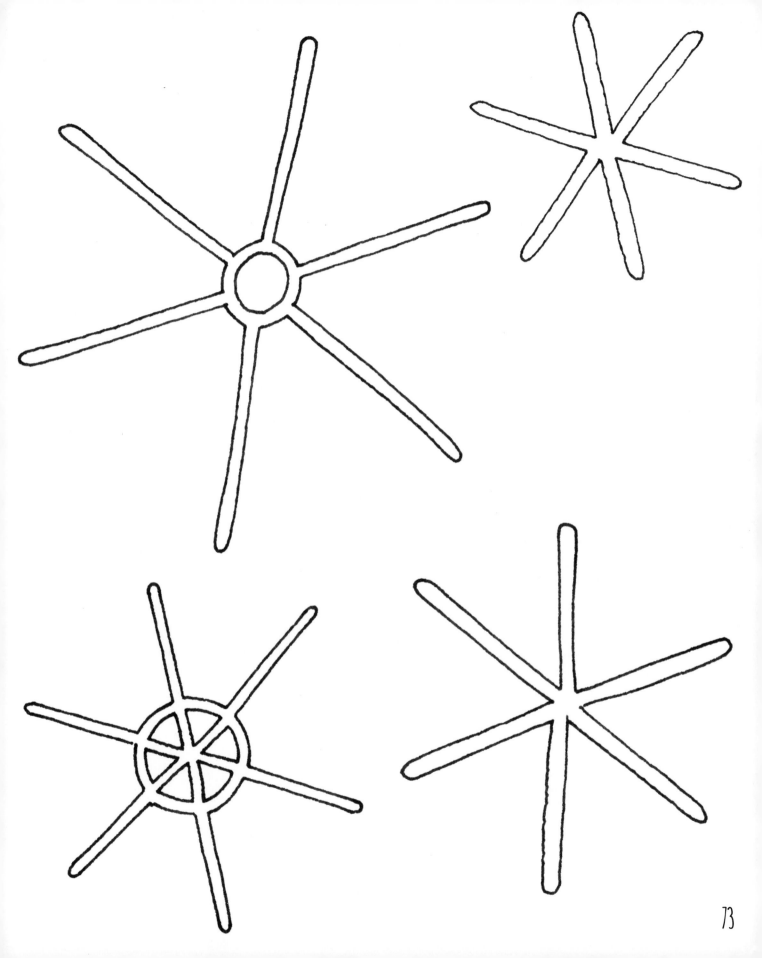

73

Imagine you're swimming underwater and you've just spied an incredible group of fish. You want to show everyone what they look like. Give each of these fish their own special patterns and colors.

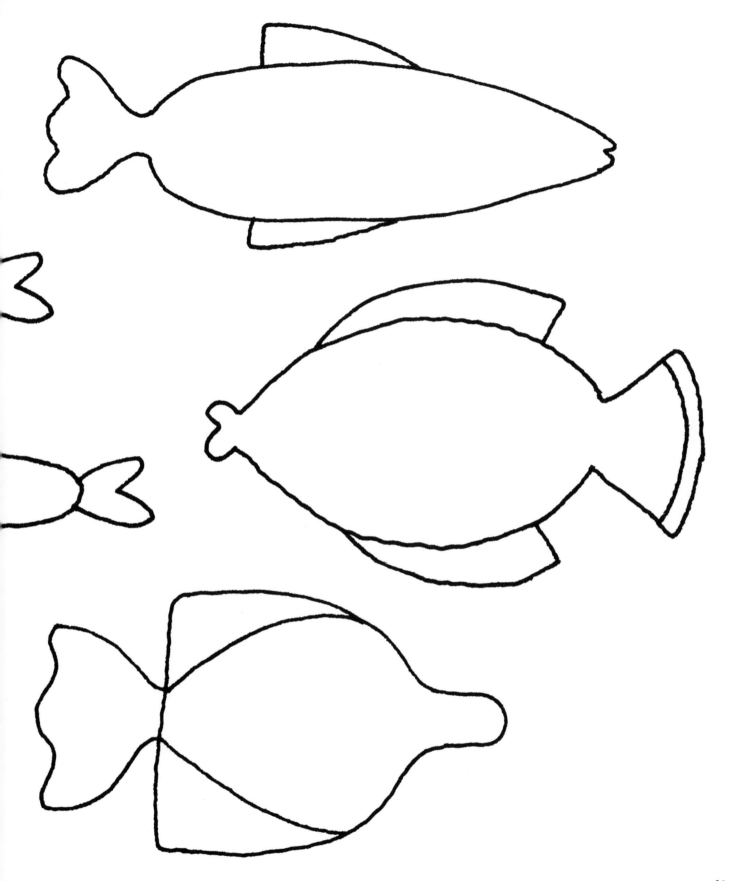

The sailboat race is on! So far only one boat is on the water. Fill the sea with boats. Each one can have its own color sail and symbol. What does your sailboat look like?

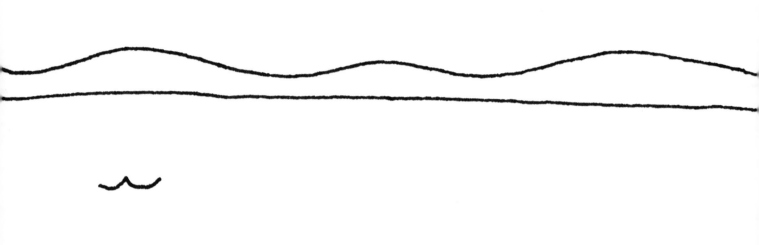

83

84

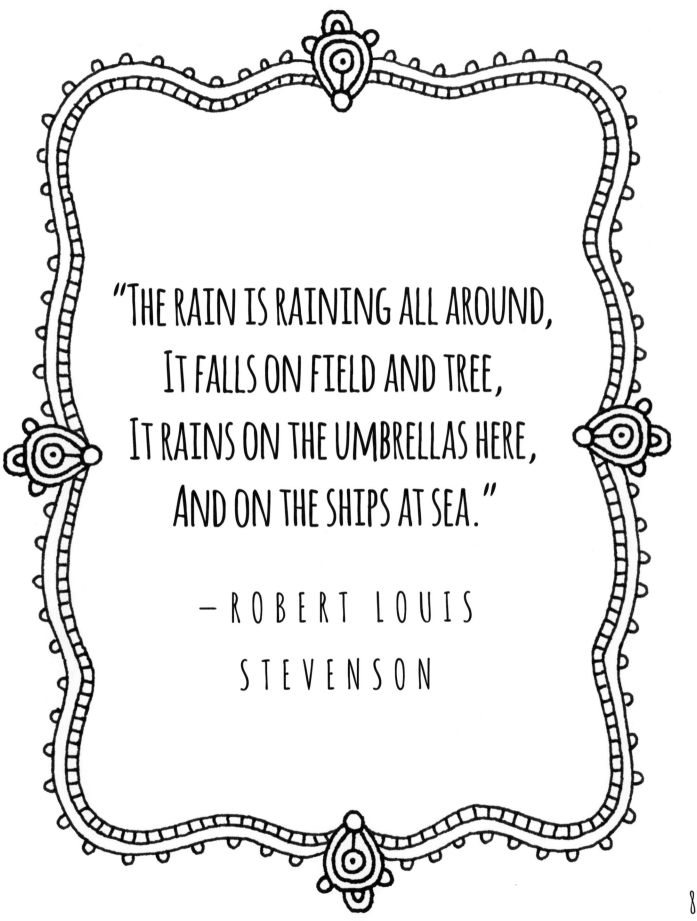

"The rain is raining all around,
It falls on field and tree,
It rains on the umbrellas here,
And on the ships at sea."

— ROBERT LOUIS
STEVENSON

NOW IT'S YOUR TURN. FILL THESE PAGES HOWEVER YOU LIKE.
WRITE, DRAW, COLOR—IT'S ALL UP TO YOU!

> *"I HEAR, AND I FORGET.*
> *I SEE, AND I REMEMBER.*
> *I DO, AND I UNDERSTAND."*
> —CONFUCIUS

LETTER TO PARENTS

As grown-ups, most of us have memories of coloring books—the first time we held one in our hands, the glossy cover containing a wealth of newsprint pages nestled inside. There was the feel of the crayon as it glided across the page, leaving a trail of waxy color in its tracks, the joy of staring into a fresh box of crayons, their sharp points and varied colors beckoning. Which picture do we want to color? Which crayons will we use?

Coloring books have been around for over 100 years. Created in 1880, they've played a variety of roles for those who have colored in their pages. Used as educational tools, coloring books teach people about different kinds of animals and plants, automobiles and ships, and so much more. They calm us, help us be patient, and act as companions, sharing our favorite heroes and heroines with us.

Now, even adults are coloring. There are a variety of coloring books available that help us slow down, relax, and reclaim the imaginative wonder of childhood. We're transported back to a time when life moved a bit slower and our imagination could unfold.

No longer left to explore the outside world after school, today's children have homework and projects, sports teams and other extra-curricular activities. The number of children suffering from anxiety and depression has gone up, and as parents, we scratch our heads and wonder how we can find time to help our children relax.

What do we do? We want our children to learn the skills they need to succeed in life, but we have to create space in which they can relax and feel comfortable with themselves, regardless of who's in the room. We want them to feel connected to their family, friends, and community.

So—how can coloring books help children learn? Coloring books are a means of helping children self-regulate. We know the clichés about coloring books—drawing by numbers or connecting the dots, they can practically be color-coded. But what if we were to see a coloring book as a guide, not as an educational tool or as an activity to simply pass the time?

That's how we invite you to see *Be Happy & Color*. **Art therapy,** sometimes called "creative arts therapy" or "expressive arts therapy," is a practice that encourages people of all ages to express and understand emotions through the artistic and creative process. Art therapy is a journey of self-discovery. When a child makes something that they can see and touch, it gives them confidence and self-control. It allows them to convey emotions and feelings that they aren't able to express with words. And when a child makes something out of nothing, with paint or paper or clay, it helps them relax; it relieves stress. Coloring can also help children cope with pain, particularly if they are experiencing illness or loss.

Kids like rhythm, regularity, and containment. Adults help children learn how to set their own rhythm when we create a life with regular times for waking up, eating meals, bathing, and bedtime.

Our hope is that by using this book, children will gain a sense of order and routine. Our vision is that these images provide a kind of meditation, so that after drawing, children feel peaceful, relaxed, warm, and secure.

Hannah Klaus Hunter

ABOUT THE AUTHOR

Hannah Klaus Hunter is an enthusiastic proponent of art therapy. She is an art therapist at the UC Davis Children's Hospital and UC Davis Hospice, working with children and adults impacted by chronic illness, grief, and loss. Hannah draws inspiration and regeneration from her own practice of art-making and shares her reflections on her blog, hannahklaushunterarts.com.

ABOUT THE ILLUSTRATOR

Artist and illustrator, Stephanie Peterson Jones works in both traditional and digital media and is known for her cheerful illustrations and patterns, intricate ink drawings, floor mandalas, and beautiful handwriting. She has illustrated many children's books, among them the award-winning *Peek-a-Moo* series, and has licensed her artwork to textile, stationery, and gift companies worldwide. Her book, *"Where's my Nose?,"* was chosen by Dolly Parton as an addition to her Imagination Library.

Before moving to Asheville, North Carolina, Stephanie and her husband, Paul, formed "Art and Kindness," a repurposed art project making decorative fish and flags from picket fences damaged in Hurricane Sandy. The couple donates a portion of the proceeds to families affected by disasters. Stephanie is inspired by beauty in nature and kind souls. When she's not making art, she's hiking, knitting, creating pottery, or teaching Pilates. To learn more about Stephanie's work, visit stephaniepetersonjones.com.